A Perfect Father's Day

A Perfect Father's Day

by Eve Bunting
illustrated by Susan Meddaugh

Boston   New York

For Sloan—an almost perfect father.
—E.B.
For H. and J.S.M., Jr.
—S.M.

Text copyright © 1991 by Eve Bunting
Illustrations copyright © 1991 by Susan Meddaugh

For information about permission to reproduce selections from this book, write to
trade.permissions@hmhco.com or to Permissions, Houghton Mifflin Harcourt Publishing Company,
3 Park Avenue, 19th Floor, New York, New York 10016.

www.hmhco.com

The Library of Congress Cataloging-in-Publication data is on file.
ISBN: 978-0-544-70900-3

Manufactured in China
SCP 10 9 8 7 6 5 4 3 2 1

4500575439

"Who's there?"

"It's Susie. And I'm taking you out for a perfect Father's Day," Susie said. "First we'll go for lunch."

"Good," Dad said.
"May I drive?"
"Certainly," Susie said.

"Have a good time," Mom called as they waved goodbye.

Susie chose where they'd eat.
"This *is* your favorite food, isn't it, Dad?" she asked.
"Sure is," Dad said. "May I pay?"
"Certainly," Susie said.

"I think we'll go to the duck pond after lunch," Susie said. "You like to feed the ducks, don't you, Dad?"

"Sure do," Dad said. "May I buy the duck food?"

"Certainly," Susie said. "And I think we'll go to the park after that."

"You like the park, don't you, Dad?"
"Of course," Dad said.

"Do you like the swings?" Susie asked.

"Do you like the monkey bars?"

"Do you like the merry-go-round? The giraffe's the best."
"I like them all," Dad said.

"Do you want a balloon, Dad?" Susie asked.
"Red balloons are my favorites."

Dad bought a red one for Susie and a blue one to bring home to Mom.

"Are you having a good Father's Day, so far?" Susie asked.

Dad smiled. "Perfect. But I think we should go home now. Mom will be waiting. Will you hold the balloons while I drive?"

"Certainly," Susie said.

Dad closed the car windows so the balloons wouldn't float away. And so Susie wouldn't float away, either.

"Mom has a special cake for you," Susie whispered. "It's chocolate with chocolate frosting and yellow writing, and it says Happy Father's Day, and there are four yellow candles, one for every year you've been my dad. It's a surprise."

"I like surprises," Dad said.

Mom was wearing her prettiest T-shirt,
the one with the sparkles that Dad liked. Their
prettiest cloth was on the table.

So was the cake.

Dad gave Mom a kiss and the blue balloon.

"My goodness," he said. "That cake's chocolate and it has chocolate frosting and yellow writing, and it says Happy Father's Day, and there are four yellow candles, one for every year I've been Susie's dad. What a surprise!"

"Dad likes surprises," Susie told Mom.
"I like chocolate, too," Dad said, and he blew out the candles and cut a big piece of cake for each of them.

"We did all Dad's favorite things and went to all his favorite places," Susie told Mom. "It has been a perfect Father's Day, so far."

"Perfect," Dad said. "May I have a hug?"

"Certainly," Susie said.